IMAGINE THAT

Licensed exclusively to Imagine That Publishing Ltd
Tide Mill Way, Woodbridge, Suffolk, IP12 1AP, UK
www.imaginethat.com
Copyright © 2021 Imagine That Group Ltd
All rights reserved
0 2 4 6 8 9 7 5 3 1
Manufactured in China

Written by Karen King
Illustrated by Marina Le Ray

ISBN 978-1-78958-597-1

A catalogue record for this book is available from the British Library

Silly Moo Moo

Written by Karen King

Illustrated by Marina Le Ray

Clonk!

One day, Moo Moo the cow was munching in her field when something fell out of the sky and hit her on the head!

'Are you all right, Moo Moo?' asked Mouse.
Moo Moo stared at him. Her head felt all fuzzy and whoozy.
'Who are you?' she said. 'Who am I?'
'I'm Mouse,' said Mouse. 'And you're Moo Moo.'
'Moo Moo?' Moo Moo frowned.

'Oh dear, my head feels fuzzy,' said Moo Moo.
'Perhaps you should go home and have a lie down for
a bit, then you might feel better,' said Mouse.

Moo Moo looked around for her home so she could lie down.
The first home that she saw was a nest in the hedge.

But she was

too big!

'Hey, this is my nest,' said Mouse.
'Cows don't live here.
Silly Moo Moo!'

Poor Moo Moo. She really wanted to lie down and have a nap. The next home that she saw was a burrow. 'Ah, that must be my home,' said Moo Moo.

But she was **too big!**

Mouse and Rabbit had to help her out.
'That's my burrow,' said Rabbit. 'Cows don't live here.
Silly Moo Moo!'

Soon Moo Moo saw a pigsty. It too looked very comfy.
'That *must* be *my* home,' she thought.
So she trotted over to the pigsty and tried to squeeze in.

But she was

too big!

'Hey, that's our sty,' said the piglets! 'Cows don't live here. Silly Moo Moo!'

Still feeling fuzzy, Moo Moo carried on looking for her home.
Soon she saw a hen house. It looked very snug.
'Perhaps that's my home,' said Moo Moo.

But, of course she was

too big!

Hen was cross.
'Hey, this is my hen house!' she said.
'Cows don't live here.
Silly Moo Moo!'

Then Rabbit had an idea.
'If we drop another apple on Moo Moo's head she might
remember again,' he said.
All of the animals thought this was a good idea.
'But how will we do it?' asked Horse.
'Leave it to me,' said Hen.

Moo Moo was still wandering around the farm when Hen dropped an apple from the roof of the barn so that it hit her on the head. Immediately, Moo Moo felt much better and set off home for a nap.

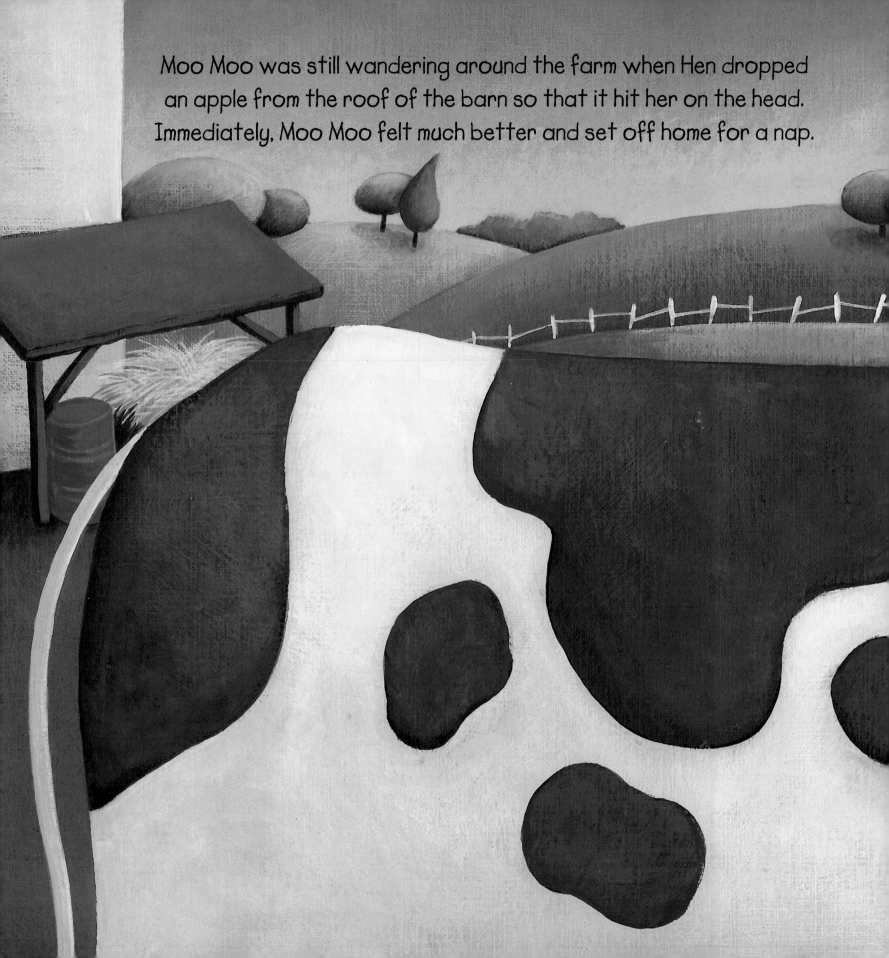

Clonk!

Later that day none of the animals
could find Moo Moo. She wasn't in her field.
So, they gathered together in front of the
farmhouse to organise a search party.
'Can anyone hear snoring?' asked Rabbit.
'It's coming from inside the farmhouse,' said Mouse.
All of the animals turned to look through the windows.

And there, on the farmer's bed, was Moo Moo. Fast asleep.

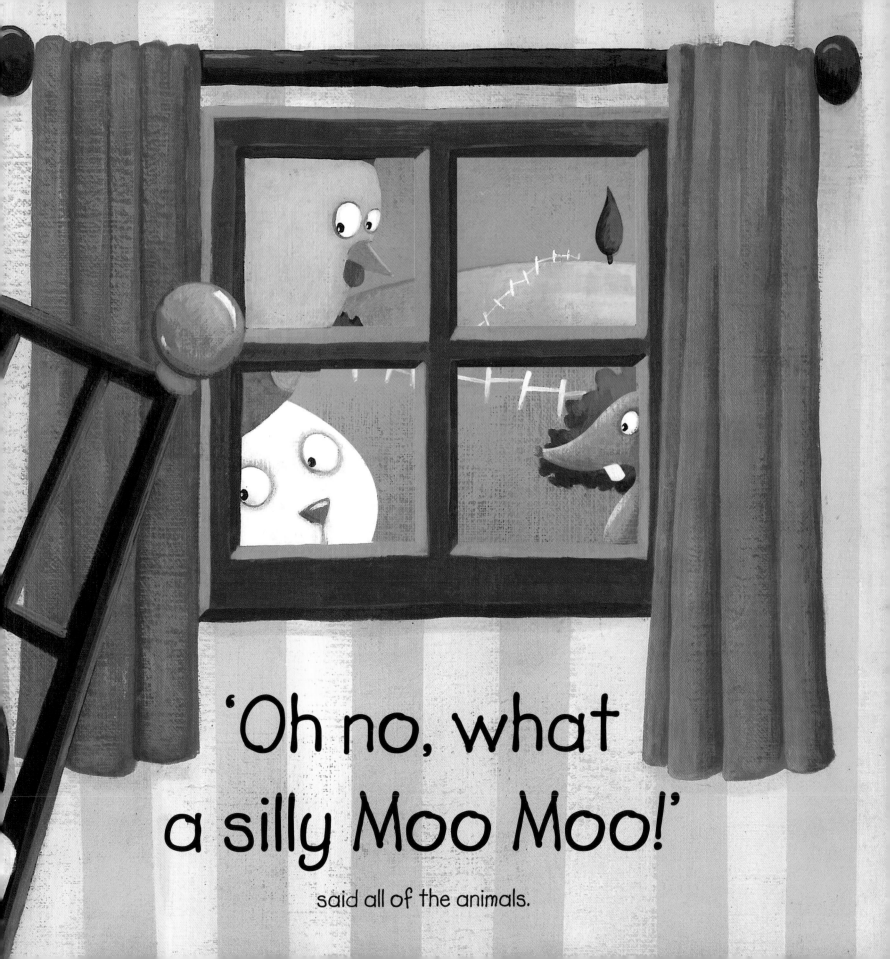

'Oh no, what
a silly Moo Moo!'

said all of the animals.